Anna M. Morrison Reed

The Latest and Later Poems of Anna Morrison Reed

Anna M. Morrison Reed

The Latest and Later Poems of Anna Morrison Reed

ISBN/EAN: 9783743369085

Manufactured in Europe, USA, Canada, Australia, Japa

Cover: Foto ©Andreas Hilbeck / pixelio.de

Manufactured and distributed by brebook publishing software
(www.brebook.com)

Anna M. Morrison Reed

The Latest and Later Poems of Anna Morrison Reed

THE LATEST

AND

LATER POEMS

OF

ANNA MORRISON REED

1896

THE HICKS-JUDD CO., PUBLISHERS,
23 FIRST STREET, S. F., CAL.

CONTENTS.

	PAGE
Across the Wire	16
" Afterwards "	14
A Golden Dream—In Memory of Leon	56
Ante-Mortem	84
As a Nun Would Tell Her Beads	68
At Twilight—Hallow-E'en	23
Browning	43
California	9
Christmas, 1890	40
Death of President Garfield—a Monody	34
Death of General Grant—a Monody	74
Easter, 1895	17
Fragments	21, 47
" Gertrude and Theodore "—a Lay of Ye Modern Knight and Lady Fair	48
Good Friday	53
Her King	31
Hurt	32
"I Do Begrudge to Time "	78
In Humboldt	18
" I Pass Her Grave "	55
" I Thirst "	61
June	50
Last Night	19
Love's Magic Seal	65
Mother—a Reverie	38
" My Life Is Devoted to Memories of You "	62

CONTENTS.

	PAGE
My Lover	22
My Treasure	13
" No Babes in Arms "—a Satire	69
Ode to Progress—Prize Poem	66
Retrospect	46
Revealed—The Vision of " Far Cathay "	11
Sacramento	82
Song—In Mexico	12
Sunset	52
"The Cup of Gold "—Bright Emblem of Our Peerless State	10
The Eclipse	63
" The Gladdest Heart "	81
Three Minstrels	15
To a Charming Portrait of a Gypsy Maiden	79
To My Beloved	64
To the Native Sons of the Golden West	60
To the University of California	73
Washington—1789-1889	42
Wasted	45
Your Life and Mine	20

PART FIRST.

THE LATEST POEMS.

TO
My Children,

In whose love and companionship I have found the greatest
happiness that life has afforded me.

ANNA M. REED.

California.

QUEEN of the Coast, she stands here emerald-
    crowned,
Waiting her ships that sail in from the sea,
Fairer than all the western world to me,
Is this young Goddess whom the years have
    found.
Ocean and land, with riches rare and sweet,
Loyally bring their treasures to her feet;
In her brave arms she holds with proud content
The varied plenty of a continent;
In her fair face, and in her dreaming eyes,
Shines the bright promise of her destinies;
Winds kiss her cheek, and fret the restless tides,
She in their truth with faith divine confides,
Watching the course of empire's brilliant fate,
She looks serenely through the Golden Gate.

"The Cup of Gold."

BRIGHT EMBLEM OF OUR PEERLESS STATE.

ACROSS the valley-land and hill,
 The south wind blows, and drones the
  bee,
Until his drowsy minstrelsy,
In fragrant chalices grows still.
Amidst a sea with orange flushed,
Like undulating waves of gold,
A million yellow buds unfold.
And like the bee, my song is hushed.
A golden noon, a golden land,
And gathered in a golden hour,
The treasure of this matchless flower,
Until at last I silent stand,
Soul-satisfied, and drinking up
The incense from each tawny cup.

Revealed.

THE VISION OF "FAR CATHAY."*

IN THIS "White City" by the lake,
  Where lilies blow and fountains play,
And swans glide through the crystal spray,
I read God's answer for the sake
Of him who suffered wrong and pain,
Yet crossed in faith the trackless main,
Where quest was stayed, nor sail was furled,
Till Christ he bore to this new world.
O spires of pearl! O domes of gold!
O arch and column—wealth untold,
Of every treasured gem of art,
Revealed you hold a a nation's pride,
The things for which Columbus died,
Because they lived in his brave heart.

---

* Columbian Exposition, Chicago, 1893.

Song.

In Mexico.

___

YES, parted, we are parted,
    And I am broken-hearted,
The southern cross shines o'er his way,
And I am broken-hearted.

He wrote: "O Love remember!
From May until December,
My heart is constant as the sun—
From May until December."

O tropic sun! touch kindly
The face I love so blindly,
Across the mesas safely guide,
The one I love so blindly.

Asunder, yes, asunder,
The sands his feet lie under,
The mescal blooms around his way,
And we are far asunder.

My Treasure.

I HAVE found a gem—priceless and rare in the
        world of men;
And all earth's hoards from bank and mine,
Where gold and silver and diamonds shine,
Could not buy from me this thing divine.
For sweeter than life—and not one breath
Can be bartered away from the tyrant death—
Dearer than fame, for which men die,
The jewel that treasure cannot buy.
No vault that stands in the busy marts
Can hold what I keep in my "heart of hearts,"
Where no rust may mar, nor bars conceal,
And thieves are powerless to break and steal.
It shines with a wonderful changeless light,
Which brightens sorrow and banishes night,
And while destiny weaves a fate untold,
It runs through the web like a warp of gold.

August, 1892.

"Afterwards."

O PALE, sweet face! Believe me—I know—I
  understand—
Even though ocean-parted, and parted by the
  land,
Longing and broken-hearted for touch of lip or
  hand.

O voice! to me the sweetest that I have ever
  heard,
And dearer than the music of wind or singing
  bird,
You need not break the silence, e'en by a writ-
  ten word.

You have blest me, and forever, by look and
  touch and tone,
And time can rob me never, nor make you less
  my own,
Although without your presence, I am bereft—
  alone.

I trust you—ocean-parted, and parted by the land,
Wild for the old caresses, of cheek, or lip, or
    hand—
I love you—O I love you! I know and under-
    stand.

In memory of Trinidad, September 3, 1892.

Three Minstrels.

THREE minstrels sing, at dawn and dark
    And through the slumberous golden
      noon—
The dove, the robin, and the lark,
Here at the threshold of the June.
At dawn the robin's matin song,
Is first to wake the dreaming notes,
And while its changes still prolong,
The Angelus rings clear and strong,
From out a myriad yellow throats.
Then as the daylight waxes dim,
The wood-dove coos her vesper hymn.
The robin at the early dawn,
The lark at noon—at dark the dove,.
Three minstrels—but the theme is love.

Across the Wire.

ACROSS the wire my darling has called to
    me to-day,
And I have read between the lines, and I know
    what he would say;
For through the formal message, which tells me
    only half,
There glows a subtle meaning, and I bless the
    telegraph.

And with this yellow slip in hand, which is
    sometimes so dread
When it brings misfortune's tidings, when it
    tells us of the dead,
I sit and dream a thousand things more golden
    than its hue,
For I love him, and he loves me, and I know that
    he is true.

Across the wire my darling from busy mart to
    mart
Has sent the words that link us, thought to
    thought, as heart to heart;
A few brief hours and by his side I'll hear the
    other half,
And know how sweet the reason why I bless the
    telegraph.

Easter—1895.

"I am the Resurrection and the Life, he that believeth
in Me, though he were dead, yet shall he live."

AT DAWN beside Jerusalem the Roman sol-
    dier paced his round
About the sepulcher; where chain,
And high priests seal securely bound,
That it might never rise again,
Dead love—Our Saviour and our King,
Who came glad promises to bring
And save from death our fallen race.

A glorious light dispersed the gloom,
And rent the rock which closed the tomb,
His first best promise kept to man,
We wait within another morn;
Forever safe from blight or ban
A perfect day, of better things,
For peace and joy and love it brings,
And we, at last, shall see His face.

In Humboldt.

ALONG the roads and sweet by-ways
　　The fireweed and golden-rod
Sway in the wind and whispering nod,
Through these long sunny autumn days.
I know the wild azaleas blow
Where every day you come and go,
Along the grades so wild and steep,
The laden vines with berries creep,
With crimson clusters in the grass
That tempt one always as they pass.

Do you remember one sweet day,
We came from Ferndale, by the bluff?
You said you'd cast the world away,
If I would say love was enough—
Without reproach—without regret—
Ah love! there's nothing I forget.

I turned away from you, and all
That might have made my life complete,
And yet no worse thing can befall,
Since we in life no more shall meet.
I chose for both the " better part,"
Which leaves me with a famished heart.

But, day by day, in fancy's light,
Through time's unceasing, restless flight,
I live; and dream of you and all
These precious memories recall—
And fain would stoop to kiss the sod
Where once we gathered golden-rod.

September, 1896.   ———

Last Night.

———

THE GLAMOUR of last night,
 Its moonlight and its dreams,
The spell that bound us waking seems
To hold me yet in long delight.
The memory of each word and look,
Still thrills me to the finger-tips,
As did your eyes and your sweet lips,
That made my soul an open book,
Its treasures bared to your dear sight.
Since you have found its mystery out,
And tenderly its secrets read,
My *truth* you cannot longer doubt;
Nor I the *loving heart* that led,
Your wandering feet to fondly trace,
The paths which brought us face to face.

Your Life and Mine.

———

SHARDS and lees after meat and wine—
   Such is your life, my own, and mine—
After the feast, the " husks and swine."

The idle word and the careless smile;
The endless tasks that the days beguile,
And hearts that almost break, meanwhile.

But you remember, and so do I,
The fond red lip and the loving eye—
These—and the thoughts that never die.

Of the twilight hush which fell so soon,
Your darling presence within the room,
A brief, sweet hour, and then the gloom.

How do I live? because I dare
Make my days but a living prayer,
That I shall find you again, somewhere.

After the storms that around us sweep,
After the toil, and the tears I weep,
Into your arms I shall sometime creep.

Hurt by the waves as they toss and swell,
Tired of the things I have done so well,
With only strength at the last to tell

How I have loved you, throughout all time;
How I have suffered, and made no sign,
True to a passion sublime—divine.

Husks and dregs after fruit and wine,
Pearls that are cast to the hungry swine,
Such is your life, my own—and mine.

---

fragment.

MY HEART has grown so heavy with the
       burden of its care,
That to Sorrow's gloomy portal I have fled and
       left no trace;
But like moths from out the darkness to the light
       of thy loved face,
My thoughts go fluttering ever from the night
       of my despair.

My Lover.

IN THE haze of the desolate desert's expanse,
  I am lost in a dream of my lover;
On the long distant lines of the hills bare and
    brown
  The flush of the sunset lies over.
The genius of light on their tops whets his lance,
  And strikes at them over and over.

I watch the long track running over the sand
  Where the swift-moving cars bore him over,
Away from the lovelight which shone from my
    eyes,
  The light that has shone for no other.
I reach out my arms and long for his kiss,
  For the lips and the eyes of my lover.

What mattered the wide, silent, sand-drifted
    waste,
  Where the wind was a merciless rover;
Over yucca and cactus and bayonet-bush,
  Where these flourish alone and no other.
The desert a paradise seemed to me when
  I was clasped in the arms of my lover.

I never again will wonder at fate;
　The strife of my life is all over;
The hunger, the longing, the weary unrest,
　Like a child on the breast of its mother;
Like a child that was lost, at last I found peace
On the passionate heart of my lover.

He will not forget me.　I read in his eyes
　The pain that none else might discover,
When he bid me good-bye with a smile on his
　　lips,
　That the truth might be known to no other.
And the desert of life will bloom like a rose
　When I next see the face of my lover.

Mohave Desert, 1893.

At Twilight.

HALLOW-E'EN.

HERE with my head on your breast,
　Here while the crickets sing,
Here let me safely rest,
　Dreaming of youth and spring.

Kiss from my face the care,
    Left there by tears and pain,
Till the brightness it used to wear,
    Shines from my eyes again.

Much have I missed in life—
    Much has my heart been wrung,
But this is a sweeter hour,
    Than poet has ever sung.

Your face is like heaven to me,
    I read in your tender eyes,
All that this world could be,
    In the radiance of Paradise.

The daylight has darkened long,
    While safe from the world apart,
I hear but the cricket's song
    And the beating of your dear heart.

O hold me close! in the gloom,
    Of the matchless hour when we meet,
In the fragrant dusk of the room,
    To die in your arms were sweet.

Tired of the world and its ways—
  Tired of its passion and strife,
And the ceaseless confusion of days
  Which make up the burden of life.

1894.

PART SECOND.

THE LATER POEMS.

TO THE MEMORY OF MY MOTHER.

Her King

A WINSOME maiden planned her life—
How, when she was her hero's wife,
He should be royal among men,
And worthy of a diadem.
Through all the devious ways of earth
She sought her king;
The snows of Winter fell before—
She walked o'er flowers of vanished Spring
Into the Summer's fragrant heat;
She bent her quest, with rapid feet,
Then saddened; still she journeyed down
The Autumn hillsides, bare and brown,
Through shadowy eves and golden morns;
And lo! she found him—crowned with thorns.

Hurt.

SOMETIMES while passing through a wood-
    land scene,
When all the world looks fair and wondrous
    bright,
Suddenly breaks a hawk's wild cruel scream,
And flies a bird, pursued, in aimless flight,
Into your very bosom, fluttering there,
While you stroke softly all its plumage torn
By beak and claw of that fierce thing of prey,
Whose murderous chase has caused its an-
    guished fright.

Bearing it home, its heart-tides quiet run,
Fades from its eyes the look of frightened pain,
Secure it preens its feathers in the sun,
And seems to be its happy self again.
Night gently comes, and underneath its wing,
Its head is folded in a trusting sleep,
Upon its breast there is no stain of red,
And yet, when dark has worn away to dawn,
The bird lies dead.

So I have come to you—
Deep in my soul an unrelenting hurt,
On your fond heart lies my defenseless head,
In your dear arms I'll shelter find awhile,
But fade from out the sunshine of your smile,
To slip away among the silent dead;
But yet I bless you for this love which bans
And would detain me in a world grown sweet;
The healing touch of your beloved hands,
That would so tenderly and deftly save
And hold me, even from the solemn grave.

Death of President Garfield

A Monody

Read in Ukiah, California, Monday, September 26, 1881.

(From the Ukiah Dispatch and Democrat.)

Mrs. Anna M. Reed then stepped to the front and read the following eloquent and most beautiful monody on the death of him who has gone from earth's scenes of toil and trouble to the realms of everlasting life, where " the wicked cease from troubling," and the " weary be at rest "; there where "the small and the great " are gathered. The reading was almost faultless, and the impression made was one of deep solemnity. The sentiments are those of a truly Christian heart, and the pathos therein contained awakened the tenderest emotions.

TOLL all the bells! a great soul's passed
    away
From clouds and shadows to the perfect day;
The wasted garment that is left behind
Must be to ashes and to dust consigned.
The tears of suffering death has wiped away,
But who shall dry the eyes of those who stay—
The aged mother and the faithful wife?
The children wailing for that ended life?
The nation calling for the leader slain,
Who long weeks languished on his bed of pain?
Toll all the bells, beat low the muffled drum;
In long procession mourning millions come
To honor him who, in a land of laws,

By lawless hand has **died,** without a cause.
Beside the ocean, that, with **measure**d surge,
Chanted his first and grandest funeral dirge—
Sublimest minstrel at the feet of God;
It still sang on, while fell the mystic rod
And moaned a requiem for the parting soul
Soaring beyond this little world's control.
No human voice may sing of him so well,
Nor all the grandeur of his history tell;
But to his memory, out of many lands,
Will struggling genius lift aspiring hands
To him who fortune's darkest frowns withstood
And kept his every aim still great and good—
Who reached the summit of the hill of fame
With life unblemished and unsullied name—
A grand rebuke to every weaker heart
That tempted, turneth from the better part;
Reproaching those who, like the one of old,
Their birthright for a "mess of pottage" sold.
His mind, untrammeled, was as broad as earth;
His heart was centered at his family hearth—
He made his home a type of all things seem
Of which the honest Christian soul can dream,
Fit emblem of that home in fairer lands

Where mansions wait, not built by human hands.
The annals of the past one truth repeat
Of those whose lives with greatness were re-
          plete—
This fact more eloquent than all beside,
Whate'er their history, they all have died.
Sceptre or crown, the pride of place or power
To frail mortality loaned but for an hour,
When death had pointed to the solemn bier,
They learned the mockery of all things here;
Sowing that others might the harvest reap,
Along the wayside they have gone to sleep—
Tired of the treasures that the years may rust,
Tired of the things that are but sordid dust,
Tired of the gold that thieves break through and
          steal,
Tired of the wrongs successive years reveal—
The graves of such, like landmarks, strew the sod,
Pointing submission to the will of God.

But though the souls of men like him we mourn
On waves of mystery are beyond us borne—
A grateful world their names perpetuate,
And well may strive their deeds to emulate;

For though they drift beyond the tides of pain
We feel indeed they have not lived in vain.
A proud inheritance has this one left

To all his loved ones and the land bereft—
His pure example may the world defy—
His glorious principles can never die;
Nor that so blessed and so heaven-sent,
On which its authors based our government,
Where earnest manhood by its simple worth,
Depends not on the accident of birth—
By honest labor, without gold to buy,
May earn and reach its stations proud and high.

Oh! let the flags droop low—toll all the bells;
We lay him down amid our last farewells.
Under the earth, with loving tributes dressed,
Do we resign him to his lasting rest;
And to Columbia, still safe and free,
We trust the honor of his memory;
As turns his sacred clay to kindred sod,
His martyred spirit finds repose with God.

Mother—A Reverie

IN THE brush fence by the lane
   I hear the stormbirds crying,
And I know the winter rain
   Soon will beat where thou art lying;
For the wind and rain are near,
   When the stormbirds are a-crying.
A brave bright winter rose
   Taps the window where I'm sitting;
Its heart with beauty glows,
   While the autumn hours are flitting;
It taps the silent pane
   Of the window where I'm sitting.
The south wind kisses light
   Its petals, curved and folded,
Like a picture warm and bright,
   Close in the heart enfolded—
Like a dream of love and youth,
   In the heart of age enfolded.
And it speaks to me of thee,
   While the stormbirds are a-crying,

Though thy face I cannot see,
  Thy memory is lying
In the winter of my heart,
  Best, brightest, and undying.
I dream of thee so dear,
  Before the woodfire glowing;
I hear the herd-bells clear,
  And the cattle softly lowing;
The sounds foretell the rain,
  While the fire is brightly glowing.
In thought I pass the lane
  Where stormbirds are a-crying,
As to some sacred fane,
  To the grave where thou art lying,
Through fragrant pine-wood aisles
  Where the sunset glow is dying;
Where one can not hear the noise
  Of a footfall on the mosses;
Where the pine leaves lightly poise
  Like a pile of russet flosses;
Where the rabbit or the squirrel,
  With silent footstep, crosses;
Where the brake, with quiv'ring fronds,
  Beside the gravestone whispers

The earliest matin songs,
  And at eve the sadder vespers,
That the night wind softly taught
  The leaves to chant in whispers.
There so quietly you sleep,
  While the restless winds are sighing.
In the grave so dark and deep,
  Nor heed the stormbirds crying,
Nor the tears that fall like rain,
  And my heart within me dying.
The rose taps on the pane,
  And the stormbirds are a-crying,
And I soon will hear the rain
  Beat through the wind's low sighing,
While rose leaves flutter down
  On the grave where thou art lying.

Christmas, 1890

WHEN, 'neath the stars of Bethlehem,
  The angels sang: "Good will to men,"
And "Peace on earth," a promise gave,
Since man was ransomed from the grave,
All earth, with sweet foreboding, smiled,
Because was born a homeless child.

A million spires point to the sky
  Where He, transfigured, took His flight,
Toward that great unsleeping Eye,
  Watching o'er death, and sin, and night,
For eighteen hundred years has been
  His triumph most devoutly sung,
O'er death, and sin, and suffering,
  In every clime—in every tongue.

Yet, while the organ grandly swells
  Within our great cathedral walls,
Chime answering chime of silvery bells,
  Upon the air of Christmas falls.
Fair women, decked in silk and lace,
  Go warm and blest to softly pray,
And hasten to each sacred place
  That gladly welcomes Christmas day.

Oh, Prince of Peace, who lived and died!
  Oh, why upon this holy morn,
When sounds and scenes of reverence tell
  This was the day that Thou wert born,
As from these temples of our pride
  The happy worshipers have filed,
Why, cold and hungry, just outside,
  Do we still find the homeless child?

Washington

1789-1889.

ACROSS a century of change
  We reach our hands to thee—
Toward one bright and changeless thing,
  Thy honored memory.

Along the battlements of Time
  No hero lived and died
Whose name in song and deathless rhyme
  Is uttered with such pride.

It stirs the hearts of free-born men,
  And whispers to the slave
The truths that e'en make eloquent
  The silence of thy grave.

No stain was on thy grand career,
  Of lust, or pride or greed;
Thy sword was never bared because
  Of some unhallowed creed.

O Washington! if from the realms
  Of perfect love and light
The immortal thought of one like thee
  May earthward take its flight,

Look down upon this land to-day—
　　Across from sea to sea—
Thy great soul will be thrilled to know
　　How much we honor thee.

We ask in thy dear name to be
　　Made faithful to our trust,
And lay our wreaths of immortelles
　　Upon thy sacred dust.

———

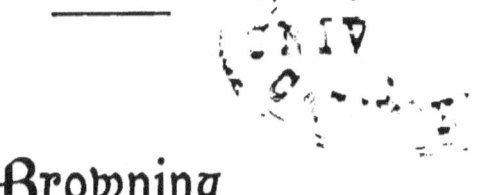

Browning

———

HE DIED in Venice—citadel of songs,
　　To which for ages all romance belongs;
At whose proud shrine the poet and the sage
Have left the offering of every age.

He died in Venice; but with dreaming eyes,
By the Rialto and the Bridge of Sighs;
And in and out a hundred water-ways,
For years he glided through the perfect days.

He died in Venice; but through all he dreamed
The golden sunshine of Italia streamed,
Where centered all those memories that endure
Around the home of Tasso and the Moor.

He died in Venice, but his work was done
Long years before his sands of life were run—
So ideal days he lived that did beseem
The closing visions of a poet's dream.

He died in Venice, where the lapping sea
Kept time to that diviner minstrelsy
With which his gifted soul through time was
     fraught
To live eternal in the world of thought.

But the worn garment that is left behind
They bear away to rest among its kind,
In that far land where, in the Abbey's shade,
Beside congenial dust, it will be laid.

A poet's love, a poet's life and death,
Blest from the earliest to his latest breath;
But of all things that could his age befall,
To die in Venice seems the best of all.

Wasted

NOT TIME, that sacred heritage to all,
 For in the cycles that have passed away
I cannot count me one lost, idle day,
Nor opportunity; to fate's most meager gift,
I have been eager, heart and hand to lift.
What waste could then my faithful life befall?

A cheek whose roses bloomed for eyes so blind,
They did not see they were the rarest kind;
Words that the world had listened for for years,
Falling unanswered on the dullest ears;
A heart worn out—as fond as ever beat,
Its wine of life spilled at unworthy feet;
A soul so tortured, as years come and go,
Its wasted treasure, God alone can know.

Retrospect

THERE is a witching mem'ry my heart so oft
    recalls—
A silver cornet ringing above the palace walls,
Where from a draperied window a bright young
    face looked down
Upon my lady's garden that graced Yokaya's
    town.

Where passion flower and jasmine diffused a
    fragrant balm;
Where shone the brilliant salvia and whispered
    pine and palm;
The willow o'er the fountain, with fingers long
    and slim,
Reached to the sparkling water that kissed the
    fretted brim,
And many a woodland songster, awearied with
    the heat,
Bathed in the cooling crystal and sang his matin
    sweet.

O days, whose dawn's pink splendor waxed to a
    golden noon !
O perfume, song and blossom, in life's impas-
    sioned rune !
O south wind, blowing gently the petals at my
    feet !
O twilight, stealing over ! O kisses, rare and
    sweet !
O little maiden, singing beside the stately hall !
O silver cornet ! ringing above the palace wall !

---

fragment

[IN AN ALBUM.]

I WILL not wish you gold, or love, or fame—
    Too many sins committed in their name,
Sweep through the ages, and with dark surprise
Their annals blast the light of artless eyes.
Virtue alone can bless and crown your youth,
Therefore I consecrate its days to truth.

"Gertrude and Theodore"

A LAY OF YE MODERN KNIGHT AND LADY FAIR.

WITH a ring of hoofs I heard them pass,
　　As the horses spurned the brittle grass;
A youth and maid of our modern time,
On the morning side of life's sweet prime.
Active and graceful, and fair and young
As any that poet has ever sung;
No knight of old, with spurs bedight
Could be to me a braver sight,
E'en though he went with plume and glove
To joust for the sake of his lady love.
And she—what maid of olden time,
Extolled in song or praised in rhyme,
Compares with her, whose form and face
Are perfect in their winsome grace?
They rode through the waning Summer's hours,
Where the sunlight sifted in golden showers
Through the woodland aisles in a solemn hush,
Through the firs and pine and hazel brush,
And down by the lessening river's brim
Where the sedge, with fingers long and slim,

Reached to the waters, clear and cool,
And dabbled in each shadowy pool.
Across their path the startled deer
Bounded away with a sudden fear ;
The grouse, from the shade of the deepest wood,
Drummed and called to their mottled brood.
Again and again was softly heard
The tender fretting of some bird
That o'er her nest, in a shy alarm,
Hovered, to keep her young from harm ;
The twittering quail to cover sped,
The silent rabbit as quickly fled.
They rode away through the pathways dim
To the redwood forest's farthest rim.
While the sun sank down in the Golden West
And rested awhile on the ocean's breast.
Into the forest, darkly dim—
I dreamed of them—she dreamed of him—
And he—not on the tented field,
Where there's only a life to take or yield—
Will this knight of mine his battle wage;
But amidst the strife of this wond'rous age,
Where swords are rusting, while gallant men
Reach nobler vict'ries by tongue or pen,

Where the proudest destiny ever sought
Is to rule a king in the realm of thought.
And what of her?—O God above!
Keep her, and shield and crown with love;
The only thing of this world a part
That is worth the price of a woman's heart.
They have ridden away through the rosy light,
Ridden away from sound and sight;
Fairer than ever was writ or sung
To the clang of hoofs their laughter rung.
Into the future dim and unknown
They will go on—but I am alone,
Dreaming of them—from the world apart—
Their laughter echoes against my heart.

June

BETWEEN the roses of the May
    Looks out the radiant face of June;
Blushing, she seems afraid to cross
    The threshold of the Spring so soon;
While my heart echoes, beat for beat,
The tread of her reluctant feet.

Passionate languor in her eyes,
　　The kiss of Summer on her mouth—
I love her harmony of birds—
　　I love her soft winds of the South—
Her cumulus clouds that grandly rise
Across the sunlight of her skies.

A lily with its laughing lips
　　Greets me, and now—a star-like shine
Thrills me from heart to finger-tips
　　With fragrance of the jessamine;
A dove her gentle note prolongs,
Answering the last late robin's songs.

As here I fondly weave my dreams,
　　While waiting—face to face with June—
Of you, my darling—beautiful
　　As bird song, blossom and perfume—
Lulled on the Summer's slumberous breast,
I dream, and know that I am blest.

Sunset

THE evening's genius with his sword of flame
    Guards well the portal of the dying day;
His lance of light he strikes against the hills,
Breaks on and glistening peaks its glancing ray;
He marshalls grandly on a crimson sea
His cloudship navy's golden argosy,
Whose flaunting banner in the sunset glow
Bids brave defiance to the dark'ning foe;
Who, swift advancing, o'er him softly flings
The purple shadow of the twilight's wings,
Till war's red flush before the night wind's
      breath
Fades out into the sullen gray of death,
And star-eyed night, prevailing all too soon,
Hangs out the silver sickle of the moon.

Good Friday

TO-DAY the Saviour died—suffered the Cruci-
    fied,
Yet could His failing eyes see the repentant's
    tear,
Saying: "In Paradise thou shalt with Me ap-
    pear."
"Father, forgive!" He prayed; such blessed
    words He said,
"They know not what they do." This in the
    face of death,
This for His enemies, asked with His latest
    breath.
Yet do His children now turn from His face and
    bow,
Not to this lowly one; down to strange gods
    beside;
And in their lust and pride, still is He crucified.

How long will they profane His pure and sacred
    name?
Placing His holy sign, His emblems so divine,
In midst of mockery, on each unhallowed shrine?

"I thirst!"—to each poor heart, struck by some
    poisoned dart,
Treading the narrow way—ready to faint and
    fall,
To the parched lips that cry, earth gives her
    bitter gall.
Oh, let us kneel to-day! kneel in the dust and
    pray,
Close to His bleeding feet; seeking our soul's
    relief,
In deep repentant grief—e'en like the dying
    thief.

Jesus, the "Prince of Peace," when shall the
    striving cease?
Dark roll the waves of death; can we the cur-
    rent stem?
Seeing at last Thy face—touching Thy gar-
    ment's hem?
Forgive each idle word Thy outraged ears have
    heard,
Each sinful act forgive; into Thy hands receive
At death our sorrowing souls, that they may
    live.
This day the Saviour died—suffered the Cruci-
    fied;

Yet He, the suppliant, heard, and He could pity-
    ing see,
Saying: "In Paradise, to-day, thou shalt be
    with Me."

"I Pass her Grave"

HERE, to and fro—Time's wearied slave—
    I come and go, and pass her grave;
A level lane—three roads divide,
Where I would fain oft pause beside,
I still pass by, on either side.

God help me! As the whip of care
    Still urges on my lagging feet,
    No time to pray, no time to greet,
And save me ere I quite despair.
    Since she is lying with the dead,
    I have no place to lay my head,
And weep for all that I have borne.
I pass her grave, nor pause to mourn;
    My heart alone stays with the dead.

A Golden Dream

IN MEMORY OF LEON.

———

"There's not a joy the world can give like
that it takes away."

WHERE the yellow Feather River
    Rolled its tide afar,
With its fruit, an orange laden,
    Grew at Bidwell's Bar.

There a little maid, one morning,
    Looking on the scene,
Tree and flower and fruit were mingled
    In a summer dream.

Steep the graded terrace—steeper
    Was the mountain side,
Where the scarlet trumpet creeper
    Trailed above the tide.

Not more scarlet was the blossom
    Than her dainty lips,
Like twin rose leaves, curved and folded,
    With exquisite tips.

And so soft and brown and changing
　Were her tender eyes,
Like a pool seen late in summer
　Where a shadow lies.

In her hands were tiger lilies,
　Gathered ere the sun
Had the time to kiss each chalice—
　Golden, every one.

As she gazed with gentle longing
　Through the lambent air,
A boy came running down the hillside,
　Crowned with tawny hair.

Blue his eyes—yes, blue as heaven,
　And his form and face
Promise bore of manly beauty,
　In their strength and grace.

O'er the garden wall he bounded,
　Plucking fruit and flower,
Tossed them to the little maiden
　In a fragrant shower.

Blushing, then, she thanked him sweetly,
  With a glad surprise
Dimpling all her smiling features,
  Shining from her eyes.

*   *   *   *   *   *   *

As she bore her treasures homeward
  Over hill and stream,
All her pure young soul was lifted
  In a sunny dream.

Through the future rode to meet her,
  On a steed so rare,
A blue-eyed prince, in royal velvet,
  With long golden hair.

*   *   *   *   *   *   *

And so shrined in her fond mem'ry,
  Lived from day to day,
Crowned with curls of rippling splendor,
  Her own prince alway.

On life's sea, uneven, drifting,
  Each the other's face did see
Seldom; and death's fiat falling,
  Parted them eternally.

*   *   *   *   *   *   *

Not one orange tree, but thousands
  Grace the plains of Butte,
And like sands upon the seashore
  Lies their golden fruit.

But one tree, where miners, delving,
  Left but seam and scar,
Crowning all the desolation
  In the past afar;

With its fruit and creamy blossoms,
  Each a separate star,
One no other tree can rival
  Grows at Bidwell's Bar.

And, alas! Time sees the passing
  Of all, good and fair—
Cold his heart—low in the grave mold
  Lies his golden hair.

To the Native Sons of the Golden West

TO THE Native Sons of the Golden West,
　　The genius of this bright century sings,
In a land where the kiss of the sun on her breast
　　Gives life to a thousand beautiful things.

Where the golden orange and scarlet fire
　　Of fragrant pomegranate blossoms shine;
Where tropical beauty and northern balm
　　Blend in the shadows of palm and pine.

To the Pioneer and the Native Son
　　Give honor, O Land of the golden West!
One's work is over, but just begun
　　For the other—for honor and fame the quest.

To the Native Sons of the Golden West
　　The Century's Genius prophetic sings—
Not alone of the past, but a future blest
　　By a countless treasure of beautiful things.

September 9th, 1890.

"I Thirst"

"Darling, you may always know that I am as
constant as the sun."

THINK you the traveler on the desert waste,
Dying of thirst, would still refuse to taste
When loving hands too gladly offered up
To the parched lips the overflowing cup?
This have I done; yet with beseeching hands,
Famished, my soul cries from life's desert sands.
As to the mirage returns the weary eyes,
Or as the lost look back to Paradise,
So to thy image, from this barren way,
My tortured spirit turns day after day.
Ere it is yielded, duty-worn and faint,
Uttering for thee its hopeless, last complaint,
Can it be sin, from this far waste of pain,
To crave some token of thy truth again?

1885

"My Life is Devoted to Memories of You"

I SAILED beneath a burning sun,
By coral reefs and isles of balm,
Where orange groves and silvery palm
By faint spice winds were gently fanned,
Until I reached a tropic land.
And with three thousand miles between
The shores whereon two oceans fret,
I bravely said, "I will forget,"
And there beneath the Southern Cross
I crept out in the breathless night;
My heart was breaking, and the stars
Shone dimly on my fevered sight—
Ah! vain is change of time or place;
In heaven itself I see—thy face!

The Eclipse

AROUND a trackless waste of sky
   A dead world haunts this world of ours,
Upon whose pulseless breast no bird
May sing in joy among the flowers—
Whence life and love and all have fled
And left it silent, cold and dead.
The only thing that still seems bright,
The blessed sun's reflected light,
The tender radiance so serene
That falls in moonlight's silvery sheen.
As on my heart these shadowy thoughts
Had left the while their sombre trace,
A shadow from the weary world
Fell over Luna's ghost-like face.

To My Beloved

YOU CANNOT come to me,
    But with this gift that God has given
I can reach out, o'er land and sea,
O'er barriers of earth and heaven,
And touch your heart exquisitely.
The bird caged with a golden wire
Sings not always for those who feed,
Supplying every grosser need;
Above the tumult of her fate
She listens, and she hears her mate;
She dreams a dream of vanished Springs,
She beats her wings, and sings, and sings—
The world says, "Sweetly sings"—but, oh!
You hear the undertone of woe.

Love's Magic Seal

OFT HAVE I smiled, when in youth's halcyon
    time,
I heard in song, or read in deathless rhyme,
How gallant knights, bedight in plume and
    glove,
Had met and fought, and gladly died for love.
How ladies, too, and maidens wondrous fair,
Had wept, and pined, and died in love's despair;
How Guinivere her crown and fame forgot,
And sweet Elaine had died for Launcelot;
How Cleopatra, on the storied Nile,
Did Antony from all the world beguile;
How brave Colonna mourned beside the sea
Her worshiped lord, till death had set her free;
How Abelard the cloister vainly sought,
And saintly Heloise her vows forgot.
Oft then I smiled; for love, in that bright hour,
Seemed to my fancy but a boasted power;
But now these things, prefiguring my fate,
    But faintly symbol all I know and feel;
This ardent passion, time cannot abate,
    Since on my soul, love set his magic seal.

Ode to Progress

PRIZE POEM

Awarded the gold medal by the Agricultural Association of Lake and Mendocino Counties, 1887.

———

GENIUS of this grand century, and guardian
    of the free,
Who can a tribute worthily bring from our hearts
    to thee?
When, 'neath the Star of Bethlehem, angels sang
    that blessed morn,
" Peace on earth, good will to all men," Prog-
    ress, thou wert also born.
The ages past had never known thee, for man
    unjust oppressed
His fellow man; who, suffering, saw might as
    right confessed.
Ask Egypt's hordes, who toiled as helpless slaves
To build her kings imperishable graves;
Or Grecian art, that on each heathen fane
Left us the dower of some immortal name;
Or Rome's imperial grandeur crumbling down,
If it was Progress marked their great renown.

No! since the world and all its works began,
Have Art and Science been the slaves of man;
Degraded oft, ignoble scopes to fill,
To suit the vagaries of the human will.
So Freedom's smile o'er Superstition's horde
Accomplished more than power of fire and sword;
While Christian liberty, o'er land and sea,
Enlightens all, and makes the poorest free;
And things that were but dreams to Greece and
        Rome,
With us to grand realities have grown.
A homeless child so touched the human soul,
He made the world akin—one wondrous whole.
His story echoes down the aisles of time,
In every language told by tongues sublime;
Nor will it cease till every land has heard
The precious promise of His sacred word,
That truth and justice shall prevail alone—
Where they are not, Progress, thou art not
        known.

As a Nun Would Tell Her Beads

WE ARE so far apart—even from ocean to ocean—

As a nun would tell her beads, only with more devotion,

Counting the days when we met,

As the chain slips over my fingers,

Over each thought of you my heart caressingly lingers.

The long, bright lance of the sun,

Reaching away from the sunset,

Touches my hair and eyes,

And the lips you kissed, when you told me,

Constant you'd always be while the sun in his shining should hold me.

The heart and the lips you love, grow warm his red rays under.

Constant I know you are, though we are so far asunder.

God bless and keep you so on the shore of another ocean—

As a nun her beads, the hours I tell, only with more devotion.

"No Babes in Arms"

A SATIRE

Suggested by seeing the above notice at the entrance to one of our
fashionable theatres.

———

WHILE Fashion trips within the door
    That Thespis opens wide before her,
Pleasure and Vice, and many more,
    Beside their goddess quickly enter,
Folly comes in, and Crime, her brother—
    All children of the same vile mother;
The courtesan, with painted charms—
But listen, not "the babe in arms."

For Innocence there is no place
    In all this grand and brilliant throng;
'Tis well, for on its modest face
    Blushes must burn for scene and song;
Or, if unconscious, still its cries
Might through the tearful silence steal,
Marring the sense of ears and eyes
    That drink the rantings of Camille.

Camille, sin-stamped, her life of crime
   Can never touch an honest heart,
E'en painted by the fingers fine
   Of sentiment and finished art,
Forgive all like her, and wish them good,
But ask not true, pure womanhood
To shed the sympathetic tear
Over her guilty, weak career.
    *   *   *   *   *   *
Over the rich man's palace gate
   Those words might well be placed quite often,
When nothing can his craving sate,
   His greed for power, and pride of station.
Some prince of style, with endless means,
   Whose social traits—a strange transition
From when he lived on " pork and beans "—
   Now swell with limitless ambition.

His wife, in fashion's trappings decked,
   Now leads a band of kindred spirits,
Of whom she is the " great elect,"
   To " kettledrums " and other places;
Forgetting how, in earlier times,
She once scoured kettles in the mines
Before she hoisted o'er her charms
The motto of " No babes in arms."

Her fragile health admits no more
   The cares that earnest woman busy;
Though grand receptions by the score
   Cannot fatigue, nor dancing weary.
" A babe so breaks a mother's rest ! "
As all her thousand friends attest,
While gossiping their usual way
Of husbands who are apt to stray,

And have a liking for their club,
   Where everybody smokes and swaggers,
While telling cronies where's the rub
   In politics and other matters.
A bad state of affairs at best,
For husbands, wives, and all the rest.

No sleep at Nature's fittest time—
   The night filled with unholy revels.
What wonder that their faces wear
   Too oft the look of heartless devils ?
And men who could have loved, at rest,
A baby on a mother's breast—
To view with interest are agog
A "thing" that pets a poodle-dog.

  *   *   *   *   *   *   *   *

The eyes of faith have looked beyond
   This life, that even at its best
Is filled with care and pain untold—
   Its triumphs filled with strange unrest,
And pictured an existence grand
And glorious in an unknown land,
Where all that pure in heart have been
As little children enter in.

While over all the hopeless dead,
   Entering at last the gates of doom,
That sentence unrevoked and dread,
   God's fiat traces in the gloom, ·
To meet and blast despairing eyes
That turn away from Paradise
And read above Hell's wild alarms:
"There enter here no babes in arms."

To the University of California

MECCA of my lost youth,
    Between thy shrine and my sad heart,
The years with pallid faces stand
    And hold us far apart.

I reached aspiring hands
    Hung'ring toward thy "mount of light";
God filled them, measuring not my plans—
    He doeth all things right.

His tasks appointed well,
    To idle heart-break not allied,
Gave nature as my "Alma Mater"
    And duty for my guide.

But echoes of thy fame
    Waft by on wings of memory,
And day by day my constant thoughts
    Like pilgrims go to thee.

Death of General Grant

A MONODY.

Read by the Author at the Memorial Exercises at
Ukiah, Mendocino County, California, August 8,
1885.

WHO HAS not stood within the chilling
    gloom
Where some bright pathway ended in the tomb,
And from its portal could no longer trace
A future—blank, for want of one loved face?
Then, dazed and broken, blindly faltering back,
Resumed the round of life's repellent track?
What family circle has not broken been
By this decree, provoked by man's first sin?
This awful mystery; whose fingers cold
Can touch impartially the young or old,
Point out the fairest for the fatal dart,
And still the beating of the noblest heart.
No pride of station and no boast of power
Prolongs a life for even one short hour.
The cottager or claimant of a throne,
On God's great mercy both depend alone;
No other power, at last, endures to save,
And all distinctions level in the grave.

Toil's implement—the monarch's royal crown,
At that dark threshold are alike laid down.
We come as beggars from the Master's hand,
And at life's close, we still as suppliant's stand—
Oh! may His mercy, like a mantle, fall
At that dread hour, in charity, on all.
What, though our burdens be of pain and care,
So great they seem, more than the heart can
        bear;
Be patient still, we all will lay them soon
Down by the portals of the quiet tomb;
And in the silence of that awful shade,
How many a fault to nothingness will fade!
The hoarded treasures of the countless years
Have been resigned before that shrine of tears.
For there, each heart has said a last "good-bye,"
And broken there is every earthly tie—
And when we hold the wreaths that triumph
        gave,
We all turn back to lay them on some grave.

*   *   *   *   *   *   *   *

What meed of praise—what tribute shall we pay
To him the nation meets to mourn to-day?
Who danger's gauntlet oft in safety ran;

Who lived a hero, but to die a man.
He was but human—but his faults were few;
His life was honest, and his purpose true.
Blame not that noble one, that fortune led
His feet where war had made the pathway red—
His country called; he did her grief assuage,
And saved America her heritage.
Where wrong has been, alone, God knoweth
     best,
And there alone His punishment will rest.
But no just thought confuses now with him
That awful scourging of a people's sin.
Over his coffin, sorrowing to-day,
Bow'd are the vet'rans of the blue and gray.
Over his grave, unworthy strife will cease,
And North and South clasp hands in lasting
     peace.
The flag, whose honor he has saved, hangs low;
And all the land is draped in signs of woe;
And many a cheek with honest tears is wet,
Now, that at last his star of life is set.
But though the flowers we bring be doomed to
     fade,
And loving hands that weave them shall be laid

To moulder back into the common clay,
Forgotten—like the tributes of this day—
He leaves one thing, that will not be forgot,
To live immortal in the people's thought.
When liberty, enlightening the world,
All false usurpers from their thrones has hurled;
When creeds no more perplex fanatic fools,
Who live by rote, and worship God by rules;
When parties die—and prejudice is dead—
And ignorance—and in their narrow stead,
A people live, by truth and reason led—
A Christian people o'er the whole earth spread—
Then will the greatness of this man be known;
Though back to dust the monumental stone
Has crumbled, his memory will shine
Throughout the ages of all coming time.
So fear not now, within the Nation's sight,
This glorious epitaph of him to write:
He leaves, emblazoned on the scroll of fame,
The matchless splendor of a deathless name.